bakery

shopping cart

vegetables

broccoli

carrot

lettuce

corn

What do you see at the park?

bench

kite

basketball court

merry-go-round

slide

playground

pavilion

What do you find at preschool?

crayons

marker

paper

teacher

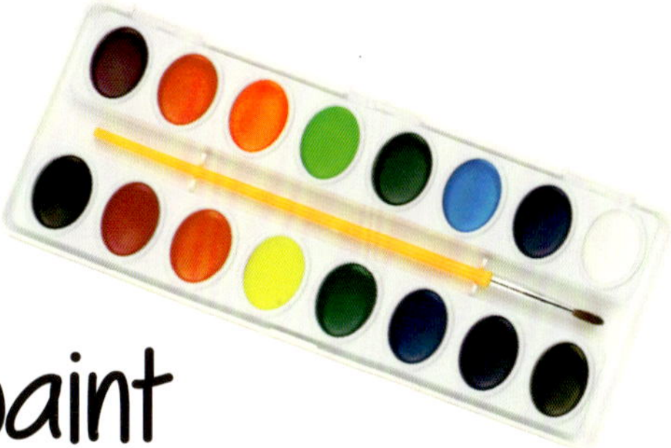

paint

classroom

desk

chalkboard

What do you find in the garden?

garden gloves

flowers

garden hose

pot

What do you see at the beach?

sunglasses

beach ball

sandcastle

sun hat

beach umbrella

shovel and pail

shells

sand

exam table

thermometer

What do you see at the doctor's office?

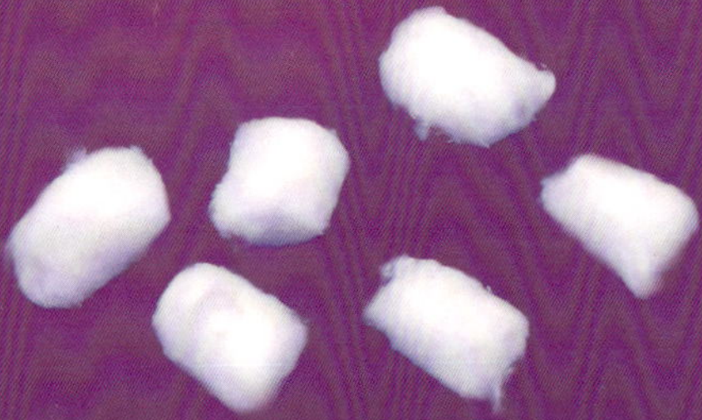

cotton balls

mask

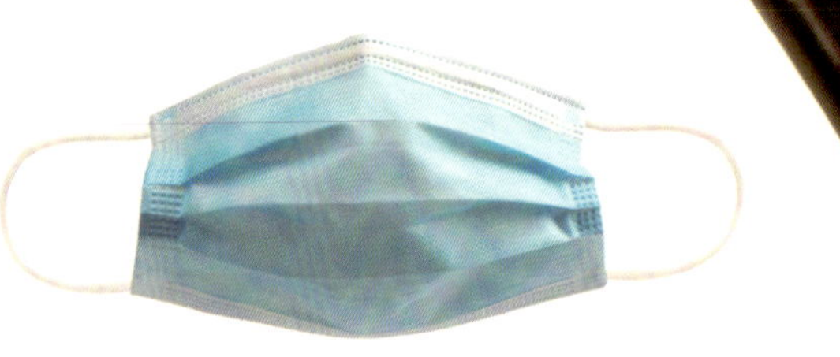

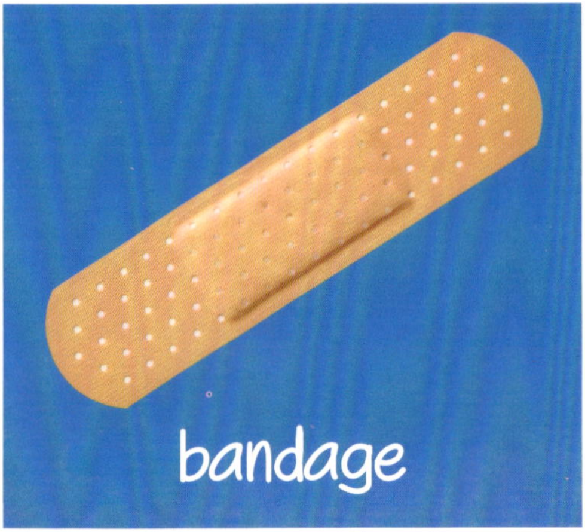
bandage

doctors and nurses

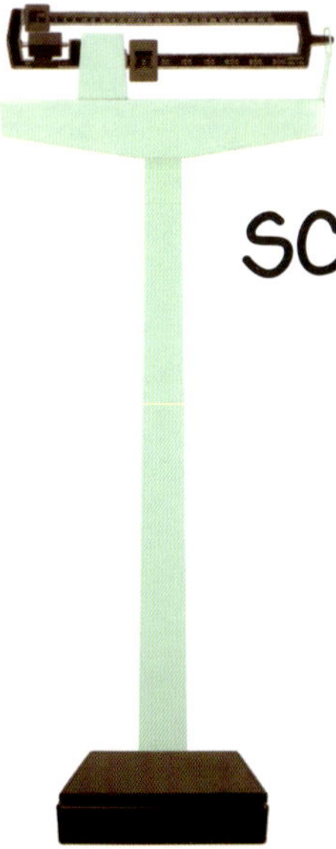
scale

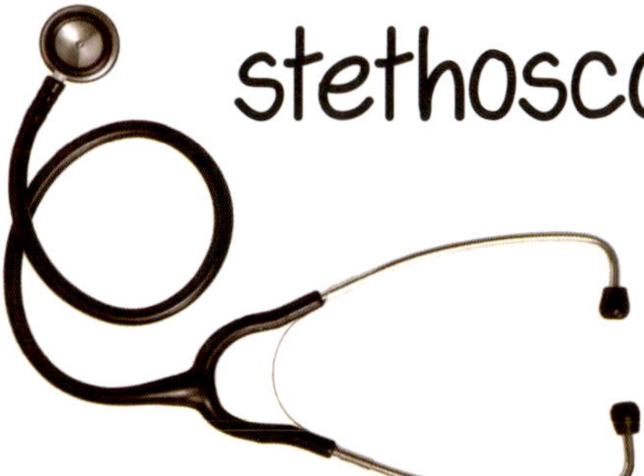
stethoscope

gloves

What do you see while hiking?

tree

leaf

trail sign

trail